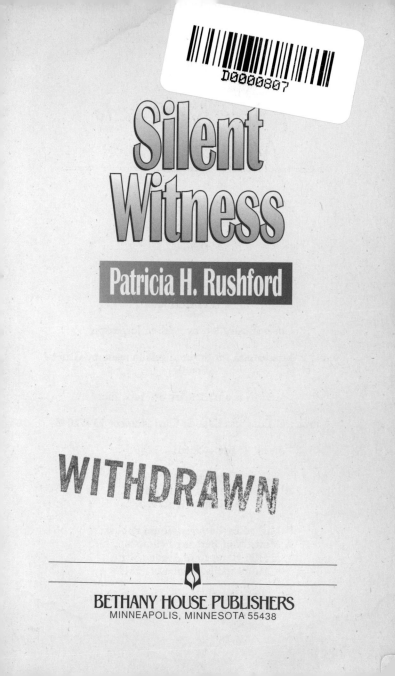

Silent Witness

Patricia H. Rushford

WITHDRAWN

BETHANY HOUSE PUBLISHERS
MINNEAPOLIS, MINNESOTA 55438

SILENT WITNESS
Patricia Rushford

Cover illustration by Andrea Jorgenson

Jell-O is a trademark for flavored gelatin made by General Foods.

M&M's is a trademark of Mars, Inc.

Library of Congress Catalog Card Number 93–72043

ISBN 1–55661–332–6

Published by Bethany House Publishers
A Ministry of Bethany Fellowship, Inc.
11300 Hampshire Avenue South,
Minneapolis, Minnesota 55438

Printed in the United States of America

Dedicated to
Kathryn, Jamie, and Michael

PATRICIA RUSHFORD is an award-winning writer, speaker, and teacher who has published fourteen books and numerous articles, including *What Kids Need Most in a Mom* and her first young adult novel, *Kristen's Choice*. She is a registered nurse and has a master's degree in counseling from Western Evangelical Seminary. She and her husband, Ron, live in Washington state and have two grown children, six grandchildren, and lots of nephews and nieces.

Pat has been reading mysteries for as long as she can remember and is delighted to be writing a series of her own. She is a member of Mystery Writers of America, Society of Children's Book Writers and Illustrators, and Director of the Oregon Association of Christian Writers Conference.

1

"A bomb threat?" Jennie stared open-mouthed at her grandmother. The authorities had delayed their flight to Orlando, Florida, Jennie's sixteenth birthday present from Gram, and had just told them why. "But who . . ." She stopped and swallowed back the fear rising to her throat. Memories of the kidnaping and the stolen diamonds flashed through Jennie's mind like a slide show.

"No," Helen McGrady said, answering her granddaughter's unspoken question. "It's over, Jennie. They can't hurt us anymore." She paused and frowned, pushing a lock of her salt-and-pepper hair from her forehead.

"But what if they escaped?" Jennie squeaked.

"You're really frightened, aren't you? Tell you what. I'll go talk with the police handling the investigation into the bomb threat and see what I can find out."

Jennie shuddered. If they'd gotten loose . . . *Stop it, McGrady,* Jennie chided herself. *There's no point in panicking. Besides, Gram's probably right. It's over.*

She uncrossed her long legs and shifted in her chair. Her legs were falling asleep from the pressure of the sleeping child that lay across them.

"No . . ." Nick whimpered and grabbed her around the neck. Jennie's five-year-old brother had been literally attached to her for the last two weeks. Separation anxiety. That's what Mom had called Nick's behavior. Jennie thought he'd been acting like a spoiled brat. But she loved him.

"Shush. I'm not leaving yet." Jennie sighed. "I just have to walk around." Except for occasional trips to the bathroom, they'd been sitting in the terminal at the airport in Portland, Oregon, for nearly two hours.

"Mom," Jennie leaned toward the auburn-haired woman who'd just returned from the rest room and taken a seat beside Jennie. "Can't you do something with him?"

Susan smiled. "Be patient with him, honey. He adores you. He missed you a lot that week you were gone."

"I know. But what's going to happen when I have to board the plane?"

"I'm going along," Nick announced. "I fixed it so you have to take me."

"You can't go," Jennie said.

"Yes I can." Nick looked entirely too pleased with himself. "I put Coco and my blanket in your suitcase and I can't sleep without 'em so you have to take me with you."

Jennie and Mom looked at each other and groaned. Coco was Nick's teddy bear. "Maybe I can intercept the luggage." Her mother stood and went in search of an airline attendant.

Nick snuggled into her lap again and rested his head on her chest. Jennie stroked his dark, wavy hair and tried to shrug off the enveloping guilt. Nick's anxiety over her leaving again had been her fault. She should have spent more time with him before she'd gone to Gram's. But Nick had seemed so attached to Michael, Mom's boyfriend, she didn't think he'd even notice she was gone.

Truth was, Jennie had been so upset with her mother and so intent on getting rid of Michael, she hadn't thought much about Nick at all. She was still upset. She did not want Mom to marry Michael Rhodes. Even if Dad had been missing for five years, and even if Michael was a nice guy, Mom had no business getting engaged. Well, maybe she did have a right, but . . .

Jennie sighed. Life could be so complicated. *Relax, McGrady,* Jennie told herself. *It'll all work out. By the end of this summer you'll have found Dad and everything will be okay.*

Gram slipped into the seat Mom had just vacated. "I just talked with the police chief, and he assured me that all of his prisoners are safely behind bars."

"It wouldn't be someone after you, would it?" Jennie asked, thinking about her grandmother's career. Gram was an ex-police officer, who now worked as a full-time writer. She also worked undercover for the FBI. Gram's friend in the Bureau, Jason Bradley, otherwise known as J.B., had assured Jennie that while Gram ran occasional errands for them, she wasn't actually an agent. But after watching Gram in action, Jennie suspected her grandmother's involvement with the FBI went considerably deeper.

Gram shook her head. "The airline official in charge said they hadn't found a bomb. The caller may have wanted to keep someone from taking the flight, but I suspect it was just a prank. They've gotten several lately."

Jennie looked in awe at her grandmother. Gram seemed to know everything, and what she didn't know she could find out.

"So what happens now?"

"They'll have another plane ready in about an hour."

"An hour?" Jennie moaned and rubbed her backside. "I can't stand it." She set Nick on the floor in front of her and stood. As she took a step forward he wrapped his arms around her leg. "C'mon, Nick, give me a break.

Why don't you sit with Gram for a few minutes so I can go to the bathroom and get something to drink."

"Nope. I'm coming with you."

Jennie sighed. "Okay, let's go find Lisa and see if she wants to come too." Nick clasped her outstretched hand and skipped along beside her.

She located her cousin in the adjoining waiting area, talking to a cute guy in a naval uniform.

"Hi," Lisa called as Jennie approached, waving her over so she could introduce her new friend, Robert, from Texas.

His plane was about to take off so the two quickly exchanged addresses and phone numbers. Robert disappeared down the ramp, and Lisa linked her arm in Jennie's and pulled her down the concourse.

"Wasn't he a doll?" she asked.

"Yeah," Jennie replied. "I guess."

"Don't sound so enthused," she joked.

"I just don't get it, Lisa," Jennie shook her head. "How can you even think about liking another guy when you're going out with Brad?"

Lisa smiled and shrugged. "Ease off, Jen, you know I don't want to get really serious with a guy right now. Besides, it's not like I'm engaged to Brad or anything."

"I know, but I don't understand how you can be in love with one guy and be attracted to another at the same time."

Lisa gave her a knowing smile and tossed back her copper curls. "It's Ryan, isn't it? I thought that about my first boyfriend too. But, after a while, you get tired of each other. You'll see. You think you've found true love with Ryan, but . . . well, face it, Jennie, guys are, you know, guys. I'll bet he's up in an igloo right now rubbing noses with some snow princess."

"Lisa, I can't believe you said that. Just because he

10

hasn't asked me to go steady and had to break our date last night . . ." Jennie paused. *Wise up, McGrady,* Jennie's inner voice insisted, *Lisa could be right. What if Ryan is already tired of you?* Thinking about Ryan tied her stomach in a bazillion knots. It still hurt. Ryan had called a week ago to say he was going fishing in Alaska for three weeks and wouldn't be there to see her off—or take her out the night before. Jennie didn't want to think about Ryan with his sandy blond hair, his tall muscular build, and his shy boyish grin. She didn't want to think about the way he'd kissed her.

Oh, for Pete's sake, McGrady, put a lid on it! Jennie shook her head.

"You're right," Lisa said, slinging an arm around Jennie's shoulder, which wasn't easy considering the fact that Jennie was nearly a foot taller than her petite cousin. "I'm sorry. I'm sure Ryan would be here if he could. Like you said, an opportunity to fish in Alaska doesn't come up often."

"Hey, I'm thirsty." Nick tugged on Jennie's belt, dragging her thoughts away from Ryan.

"Hi, Thirsty, I'm Jennie," she teased, glad for the disruption. She took his hand and pumped it. "Nice to meet you. How'd you get a name like Thirsty?"

Nick giggled. "It's not my name, silly. Now quit joking me and let's go get some pop."

Not wanting to resume their conversation about Ryan, Jennie told Lisa what Gram had said about the bomb threat.

"Wow. That is so scary," Lisa said as she took hold of Nick's other hand. "I mean, what if they missed it and there really is a bomb?"

"I guess that's why they're putting us on another

plane." The girls stopped talking as Nick raised his legs and swung between them.

"Swing me higher," he pleaded. They swung Nick back and forth between them until they reached the snack bar. While Jennie and Lisa slowly made their way back to the waiting area, Nick surprised them by running ahead.

"Whew, I was beginning to wonder if he'd ever let go of me. I hope he doesn't have too hard a time with my leaving this time."

"He won't." Lisa took a sip of her drink. "My mom's taking Kurt to your house after his Little League game to sleep over tonight." Kurt was Lisa's little brother. And Lisa's mom, Kate, was Jennie's aunt—Dad's twin sister. They had this complicated family where it seemed as if everyone was doubly related to everyone else.

"Everything will be fine," Lisa assured. "So quit worrying and start thinking about all the gorgeous guys you're going to meet. I wish I could go along."

"I wish you could too. But you know how Gram is. She likes taking one of us at a time. Besides, I'm the one who should be jealous. You get to go with Gram on a cruise for your birthday."

Lisa grinned. "I know. Look out Love Boat, here comes Lisa Calhoun. I'm planning on meeting the man of my dreams." She sighed and broke into a dance that reminded Jennie of Claire in *The Nutcracker*. Jennie rolled her eyes and grabbed Lisa's arm just as she was about to crash into a couple standing near the waiting area.

As they passed the couple, Jennie overheard something that brought her to an abrupt halt.

"Maggie," the man pleaded, "please don't do this. What if that bomb scare was meant for Sarah?"

2

"Jennie?" Lisa had walked a few feet ahead and turned to look back. "What . . ."

Jennie shushed her. "Did you hear that?" she whispered. "That guy thinks the bomb threat might have been meant for Sarah."

"What guy, and who's Sarah?"

"The guy with the brownish hair and mustache. He's standing next to Maggie. She's the woman in the expensive denim jacket and designer cowboy boots. I don't know who Sarah is, but I'd like to find out." Jennie pulled Lisa down into some chairs near the couple.

The woman, Maggie, must have been arguing with the guy because he took hold of her shoulders and said, "Honestly, Maggie, sometimes I'd like to throttle you. You can be so stubborn."

"Apparently it runs in the family."

"Did it ever occur to you that Ramsey might not have killed John?"

"The police are satisfied."

"The police have so much work, they're satisfied with just about anything that seems logical. Well, it doesn't seem logical to me. It never did."

Maggie made a choking sound and fumbled in her

pocket for a tissue. "Oh, Tim, we've been over this before. Don't you see, I need to put all that to rest. What matters now is getting Sarah well. And if this new therapy works . . ."

"If this works, she might remember . . ." Tim pulled Maggie into his arms. "I'm sorry. I didn't mean to upset you. It's just that I . . . well, you know how I feel about it. And you're probably right. I'm letting my imagination run wild. Just promise you'll call me if you see any change in Sarah. I want to be there."

"Attention, please," the ticket agent announced. "We'll be boarding flight 334 in just a few minutes. At this time we'd like those passengers who need assistance in boarding to come to the gate."

"Darn." Jennie watched as Tim and Maggie hurried into the waiting area. Maggie stepped up to a wheelchair and leaned toward it.

"Time to go, Sarah." Another man with hair so blond it was almost white took hold of the wheelchair handles and turned it around, nearly running into Jennie, who'd positioned herself next to the group, hoping to learn more.

His light blue eyes met hers and crinkled at the corners in a smile. He apologized and quickly swung the chair in the direction of the gate, but not before Jennie got a good look at the girl sitting in it. So that was Sarah. A chill shuddered through Jennie. Sarah had a look in her eyes that Jennie had never seen before—a sort of hollow, vacant look, and something else she couldn't quite place. Fear?

The foursome stopped near the ticket agent. Tim stooped to kiss Sarah's cheek, then gave Maggie another hug. "Don't forget to call."

14

The blond man patted Sarah's hair and kissed her cheek. "Get well, Princess," he said as he straightened. He pulled Maggie into his arms and kissed her on the lips. "I wish I could come with you today, but my clients . . ."

"They need you. Besides, it'll only be a few days. We'll manage until you get there." Maggie kissed him again, turned and walked with Sarah into the tunnel.

Jennie felt as if she'd been watching a rerun of *Casablanca* and *Heidi* rolled into one. Based on the kiss, she decided Maggie and the blond man must have been married, and Tim? Maybe he was a brother or something. As she watched the men move out of the gate area and down the concourse, Jennie had an uneasy feeling about them. The chill she'd felt earlier settled into a ton of questions that sat in the pit of her stomach like lumps of undigested food.

Before Jennie had a chance to consider what she'd just witnessed, Gram put a hand on her shoulder. "It's time to go."

Jennie turned toward her mom and Nick. Mom, of course, was crying. "You have a wonderful vacation, and be careful. Call me. And try to keep your grandmother out of trouble, will you?" She said it in a teasing way, but Jennie knew she was halfway serious.

"I will, Mom. And don't look so worried. We'll only be gone a couple of weeks."

Mom sniffed. Gram hugged her. "Don't you worry about a thing, Susan. We'll be fine. As I told you before, we're just going to do some research on dolphins for a series of articles I'm writing."

Lisa embraced Jennie and Gram in a group hug. Gram reached for Nick. "You don't have to hug me, Gram," he

15

announced. "I'm going with you guys."

Jennie picked him up and held him close. "Sorry, pumpkin. You have to stay home this time."

"No, I'm going. I have to. Coco and my blanky . . ."

"Jennie will mail them as soon as she gets there," Mom told him, then to Jennie said, "I couldn't intercept them. Federal Express them the minute you get to the hotel."

"I will. I'll be back before you know it, Nick." Jennie tried to hand him over to Mom, but Nick had a stranglehold on Jennie's neck. "I'll bring you back all kinds of neat pictures, and I'll tell you all about the trip."

"No!" Nick screamed in Jennie's ear. Mom reached up and they managed to untangle Nick's arms and legs. From the way he was kicking, Mom's legs would be black and blue by morning.

"You two better go before your plane leaves without you," Mom said. "He'll be okay." Nick had now attached himself to Mom and was sobbing inconsolably into her shoulder.

"Do you really think he'll be all right, Gram?" Jennie asked as they made their way down the ramp. "I've never seen him this upset."

"He'll be just fine. I'll bet by the time we get seated, he'll be standing at the window waving goodbye."

Jennie smiled. If Gram wasn't worried about Nick, she wouldn't be either. As they stepped into the plane and made their way through the first-class seats, Jennie spotted Maggie and Sarah. Maybe she'd have an opportunity to talk to them during the flight, or during their layover in St. Louis, and find out why Tim thought the bomb threat had been meant for Sarah. Jennie followed Gram down the narrow aisle to their seats. Just about the time they'd stowed their carry-ons and squeezed into their seats, the person occupying the window seat showed up so they had to shift and start the process all over again.

When the plane backed away from the terminal, Jennie leaned forward in her seat on the aisle to see if she could spot Nick. Gram had been right. He was waving. Jennie waved too, knowing he couldn't see her, but knowing too that Mom would tell him she was.

The woman seated next to Gram was a teacher, and she and Gram talked nonstop for the first hour and a half of the flight. Jennie tuned them out and tried to concentrate on her latest mystery book. The girl in the story had been kidnaped, and Jennie could identify all too well with her. When the meals came, Jennie took the opportunity to tell Gram about the conversation she'd overheard.

"Oh, I wouldn't worry about that," Gram said as she removed the foil cover on her chicken entree. "Bomb threats frighten people, and they start thinking about possibilities in their own lives. We did it, remember. The first thing we thought about was who would want to hurt us."

"But they were talking about a murder."

"Yes, well unfortunately, murders aren't that rare today—especially in Portland."

Annoyed that Gram didn't find her discovery as enticing as she did, Jennie took a bite of what was supposed to be potatoes, and grimaced. It tasted like flavored cardboard. Too hungry to care, Jennie swallowed it and tried a bite of the chicken. That, at least, was edible.

"It probably doesn't mean a thing," Gram turned back to her. "But, just to satisfy your curiosity, why don't you see if you can talk to them?"

As soon as she finished her meal and the carts had

vacated the aisle, Jennie slipped out of the seat. It felt good to stretch. Even though Gram had given her the outside seat, she felt like one big cramp. Jennie made her way to the bathroom located at the back of the first-class section.

While she used the facilities, Jennie rehearsed what she'd say to Maggie. Should she get right to the point? "Excuse me, but I overheard you talking about the bomb threat and a murder and was just curious . . ." *Get real, McGrady, an opening like that would probably get you ejected from the plane. Not a pleasant experience at twenty thousand feet. Maybe you could just ask her about Sarah.* "Excuse me," she could say, "I couldn't help noticing that your daughter seems a little strange." *Strange? Maybe you should forget it, McGrady. It's none of your business, and after this flight you'll probably never see them again anyway.*

She wasn't sure why, but Jennie was more nervous than she'd been when she'd had to read her history report in front of the entire junior class. Her palms were sweating, and she felt as if a thousand butterflies were about to take off in her stomach. Jennie eased out of the cubicle and stepped into the first-class section.

"Can I help you?" Jennie whirled around and came face-to-face with a smiling flight attendant.

"I . . . ah . . ." The butterflies took off. "I was just . . ." Jennie broke off as she noticed she was standing next to Maggie and Sarah's seats. They were both sound asleep. Jennie smiled back at the woman. "I was going to talk to Maggie and Sarah, but they're sleeping. Maybe I'll try later."

The flight attendant nodded. "Do you want me to tell you when they wake up?"

"No . . . I'll catch them during the layover in St.

Louis." Jennie made her way back to her seat and folded her lanky body into her allotted space. "I think I'll design airplanes when I grow up," she said to Gram. "The first thing I'll do is put in wide seats with lots of leg room."

Gram, Jennie, and their seatmate talked for a while about developing the perfect airplane, and in what seemed like only a few minutes, the pilot announced their arrival in St. Louis.

By the time Jennie and Gram emerged from the tunnel, Maggie and Sarah had disappeared. *Give it up, McGrady,* Jennie told herself. *Think about Gram. You're here to spend time with her, not to try and solve another mystery. Besides, the last one should have cured you.* But it hadn't. Jennie had to admit that after the diamond caper, even though she had come close to losing her life, she was more into solving mysteries than ever.

Jennie resolved not to think any more about Maggie and Sarah. Instead she would concentrate on two things—talking Gram into finding Dad and having a good time in Florida. Make that a *great* time.

3

Even though Jennie had decided not to think any more about Maggie and Sarah, she couldn't help looking for them as she and Gram hurried through the St. Louis terminal. "It just isn't fair," she muttered as they waited in line to board their flight.

"What isn't fair?" Gram looked up from the newspaper she was reading and slipped her reading glasses down on her nose.

"Maggie and Sarah. Those people I was telling you about. I admit I'm really curious about them, but there's something more. I can't stop thinking about them. And, well . . . I can't explain it, but I have this eerie feeling that Sarah's in danger. And now they're gone."

"And you feel frustrated because you were hoping you could help?"

"Yeah. I don't know how, but maybe you and I . . ."

Gram smiled. "You and I are very much alike, Jennie. I meet people nearly every day who are in need or troubled. I wish I could help them all, but it's simply not possible."

"Are you saying I should forget about them?"

"No, not forget, exactly. But you might think about doing what I do."

"What?"

"I pray." Gram folded her paper, set it aside, and removed her glasses. Jennie cringed. Gram was about to share one of her "theological insights." That usually meant an in-depth discussion on something Jennie didn't especially want to hear. But Jennie indulged her, partly because what Gram had to say usually made sense, but mostly because she adored Gram and didn't want to hurt her feelings. Gram's deep blue eyes turned thoughtful. "You see, Jennie, I don't think anything happens to us by chance."

"You mean, like there's a purpose for everything?"

Gram nodded. "God often gives us glimpses into other people's lives. You may never have the chance to talk to them, but you can help by praying for them. Sometimes that's the only help we can give."

The ticket agent called for passengers to board, and as Jennie made her way through the gate and onto the plane, she did pray for Maggie and Sarah, especially for Sarah. *God, I don't know what's going on, but keep her safe.* Then as an afterthought Jennie added, *. . . and if it's all the same to you, could you let me see them again so I can find out what this murder thing is all about?*

This time as they took their seats, Jennie was pleased to see that she and Gram occupied the only two seats on their side of row fifteen. No seatmate. That meant Jennie could talk to Gram about finding Dad. As she rehearsed what she'd say, the butterflies started in again.

For Pete's sake, McGrady, Jennie lectured herself, *this is your grandmother. What are you nervous about? Just tell her how you feel about Dad being alive, then ask her to help you find him. What's so hard about that?* But Jennie wasn't nervous, she realized. She was afraid. She'd been waiting for just the right time to talk with Gram, and this was it. But what if Gram said no?

Jennie glanced over at Gram and gave her a weak smile.

"Did you want to talk about Maggie and Sarah some more?" Gram said gently.

"No," Jennie answered. "I just . . . I was just thinking about how much my dad looks like you." That wasn't exactly what she'd meant to say, but as the words escaped her lips, she realized how true they were. Even though Gram's skin was wrinkled and her hair had turned gray, there was something about her expression and her eyes.

Gram's smile vanished, and her deep blue eyes clouded with tears.

Nice going, McGrady. "I'm sorry," she mumbled and turned away.

Gram put a comforting hand on Jennie's arm. "It's all right. I always get teary when I think of Jason . . . your father. I don't think a parent ever gets over losing a child. Even when they're grown. If you want to talk about him, it's okay."

"I don't want to just talk about him. I want to find him." Jennie groaned inwardly. *So much for diplomacy. Well, now that I've jumped in, I might as well keep swimming.* "What I mean is, I . . . well . . . Mom is going to marry Michael and I have to find Dad so she won't."

"Oh, my dear girl. I had no idea you were so unhappy about your mother and Michael. You seemed to be handling it so well." Gram took hold of Jennie's hand. "Maybe we better talk a little more about this."

Jennie took a deep breath and tried to organize her jumbled thoughts. "Okay. It isn't just about Mom and Michael. I've been wanting to search for Dad ever since

22

he disappeared. I miss him so much. You know how you always said you felt that Dad was alive? You said what happened to Dad was like a story without an ending. You still feel like that, don't you?"

Gram leaned back against the seat and closed her eyes. Jennie's chest felt tight and she couldn't breath. *She's going to say the same thing Mom and Aunt Kate said, that Dad is dead and I need to accept the fact. She's going to say no.*

"Yes," Gram whispered and opened her eyes again. "Yes, I do."

Jennie let out the breath she'd been holding. "Then you'll help me find him?"

Gram shook her head. "I didn't say that. Jennie, I understand how you must feel. After his disappearance I hired private detectives and had every law enforcement agency in the country looking for him. We hit nothing but dead ends. All we have is a record of the flight plan he filed and a tape of his mayday call to the Sea-Tac tower."

"So you've given up too?" Jennie pulled her hand away and folded her arms against her chest.

"I'll never give up completely, but I just don't think it would do any good to launch another investigation."

"Well, I have to. And if you won't help me, I'll just have to do it myself. Maybe J.B. will help. He said he thought Dad was still alive."

"You're really intent on doing this, aren't you?"

Jennie nodded. "I want my dad back. And I have to stop Mom from marrying Michael."

"Even if we could find your father, I doubt . . ." She hesitated, but Jennie knew what she'd planned to say.

"I know, there's no guarantee that Mom will take him

23

back." Mom hated his working for the FBI, hated the danger and the days and weeks when he'd have to be away from home working on some important assignment. Mom had never understood how important that work was. Jennie reached out and placed her hand on Gram's arm. "I know it probably sounds crazy, but I have to try."

"Well, I can't promise anything, but I will talk to J.B. about it when we get home. It's been a while . . . who knows, something may have surfaced."

Hope ballooned in Jennie and she burst into a wide grin. "Thanks."

————————

As soon as they reached the hotel, Jennie rescued Nick's blanket and Coco from her suitcase and arranged with the manager at the front desk to Express Mail them back home. Back in her room she placed a call to Nick and her mom to let them know the valuable cargo was on its way. After assuring Mom that everything was fine, she talked to Nick.

"Hi, little buddy. How are you feeling?"

"Fine. Michael's playing horsey with me. Kurt's here and we're gonna watch *101 Dalmatians* and have pizza and everything."

"I miss you, pumpkin, but I'll be home before you know it."

"Okay, I gotta go. Bye."

Jennie was glad he'd gotten over her leaving, but at the same time felt a twinge of disappointment. He could have at least said he missed her too. *Quit acting like a baby, McGrady. You should be thankful he's okay.*

She talked with her mom for a few more minutes, then donned her blue Speedo swimsuit, a matching cover-up,

24

and thongs. "Want to join me at the pool, Gram?" Jennie called through the bathroom door.

"Sounds great, but I need to make some phone calls first. You go on ahead, I'll be down in a few minutes. Oh, here," Gram opened the door, "you'll need this." Jennie grabbed the thick white towel and headed for the Olympic-size pool in the hotel courtyard. Orlando was a balmy eighty-three degrees, and even though it was getting dark, Jennie didn't want to waste a minute of her Florida vacation.

The next morning, in shorts, sandals, sunscreen, and sunglasses, Jennie and Gram headed south. They reached their first stop around noon—Dolphin Playland on Miracle Key, near Key Largo. They grabbed a quick lunch at the theme park's adjoining restaurant and resort. Part of Gram's interview was to tour the facilities and watch the sea lions and dolphins perform. Jennie had been invited to join them. As they made their way toward the park entrance, they encountered six demonstrators carrying picket signs. A young woman in torn, faded jeans and a pink tank top and a shirtless guy in tattered cutoffs approached Jennie and Gram. The woman, probably college-age, carried a sign that read, STOP EXPLOITING DOLPHINS. The guy's sign read, DOLPHIN KILLERS.

"Hi, I'm Melissa and this is Scott. We're with the DPA—that's the Dolphin Protection Agency. You might want to read this before you go in." She handed them each a flyer.

Jennie scanned the paper titled, "Dolphin Killers." Under the heading was a newspaper article about a dolphin named Maria who had died at Dolphin Playland from unknown causes. The flyer went on to say the DPA suspected foul play. The dolphin had been disposed of before the agency could do an autopsy.

Jennie looked up and found Scott scowling at her. "You're going in there anyway, aren't you?" He stepped forward, his face only inches from hers. His sea-green eyes flashed with anger.

Jennie backed away. "I . . . ah, my grand-mother . . ."

"People like you make me *sick*," Scott went on. "All you care about is having a good time."

"That's not fair," Jennie flashed back. "You don't know anything about us." She straightened to her full height and faced him eyeball-to-eyeball. The brief look of surprise on his face told Jennie he wasn't as tough as he appeared.

"Yeah? Show me. I'll bet you ten bucks that you go in, even after reading that article."

"Yes." Gram put a hand on his arm as if to draw him away from Jennie. "You're absolutely right, young man. She is going inside." Gram handed him a twenty-dollar bill. When he didn't take it, she took hold of his hand and stuffed the money into his fist. "We both are."

Scott opened his mouth to protest, but Gram contin-ued. "We're going in, but not for the reason you think." Gram introduced herself and Jennie and explained why she was there. "I'm gathering information, pro and con, about dolphin research. Then I will put together what I feel are fair and honest articles. Now, if you'll excuse me, I'm late for my appointment."

"I'm sorry for the hassle, Mrs. McGrady," Melissa said. "Scott hasn't been with us too long, and he tends to get carried away."

"So I see. Well, young man, if you think you can hold your temper, I'll be happy to sit down with you when I'm through here and listen to your side in all this."

Scott seemed surprised at her offer. "Th . . . that would be great."

"Then, I'll meet you here at about two-thirty."

"Oh . . ." His eyes clouded, reminding Jennie of fog settling on the ocean. "I can't . . . I have to get back to Key West—I work for Waterworks Cruises and have to take the sunset cruise tonight."

Gram smiled. "That's fine. We'll be staying in Key West for the next couple of nights. You can reach me at this number." Gram scribbled the number on the back of one of her business cards and handed it to him. When he reached for it, the twenty-dollar bill fell to the ground.

"Oh," he flashed Gram an embarrassed grin. "I forgot I had this. Here . . ." He scooped it up and handed it to her. "I guess you'll want it back."

"Keep it." Gram held up her hand. "Consider it a donation to the DPA."

Melissa and Scott both murmured thank-you's as Jennie and Gram made their way into Dolphin Playland.

"He's a nice boy, don't you think?"

"Nice?" Jennie grimaced. "He's obnoxious and arrogant and . . ." She turned back. Scott was still watching her. Their gazes met, and Jennie felt a fluttering in her stomach. She turned abruptly and followed Gram inside. *Good grief, McGrady, have you lost your mind? The guy's a total jerk.* But despite his less-than-charming personality, Jennie realized she was looking forward to seeing him again.

4

At two-thirty Jennie and Gram passed through Dolphin Playland's exit bars. The protesters still stalked the entrance, handing out brochures and trying to talk people out of going inside. Scott and Melissa were gone.

"I still don't see what the big deal is," Jennie said. "I mean, it's no different than Sea World or a zoo. It's fun and educational to see the animals and pet them. I had a great time."

"It was fun," Gram agreed. "Although I wasn't too crazy about petting the sharks. I loved watching the dolphins and sea lions perform. And they seemed to be having as good a time as the audience."

"From the way Scott and Melissa were talking, I wasn't sure what to expect. I still can't understand what the protesters are so upset about."

"I guess we'll just have to ask Scott." Gram unlocked the car they'd rented, a white LeBaron convertible. "Would you like to drive for a while?" Gram asked. "I'd like to go over my notes." At Jennie's enthusiastic yes, she handed Jennie the keys and climbed in the passenger side.

"Where to?" Jennie asked as she followed the arrows leading out of the parking lot.

"Just get on the main road and head south."

Jennie giggled. "I know that. I meant where's our next stop?"

"Grassy Key. The Dolphin Research Center there. We'll go on a tour and talk briefly with the director. I really wish I had more time to spend there. It's one of the best dolphin research centers in the country."

"So why aren't we staying longer then? We've got two weeks."

"The program there is similar to the one on Dolphin Island up near Fort Myers. The directors are good friends and have invited us to stay as long as we want for free. That way I'll be able to get a real feel for what dolphin research is all about. I think what will be most fascinating is seeing how dolphin therapy works firsthand."

Jennie eased the car onto the freeway, then asked, "What's dolphin therapy?"

"Basically, it's using the dolphins and the way they interact with humans to treat people who might benefit from it. Some psychologists feel they can be helpful in treating certain clients."

"Oh, yeah. You mean like that little boy with Down's syndrome in the article you gave me. His mom said since she started bringing him to the dolphin center he's gotten a lot better. I saw the show on one of the news programs too. That was so cool."

"He's making dramatic strides." Gram reached back for her lap-top computer. "And while I'd love to chat more with you about it, I think I'd better get my impressions of Dolphin Playland down before I forget. We'll be able to watch some therapy sessions firsthand when we get to Dolphin Island."

Gram settled into writing and Jennie into driving. Actually she was glad for the silence. Except for the traffic through the towns, this was one of the most scenic roads Jennie had ever driven. The highway stretched from key to key between the Gulf of Mexico and the Atlantic Ocean. As she passed one small, isolated island accessible only by boat, Jennie wondered what it would be like to live there. She'd never known anyone who owned their own island. *It'd be wonderful,* she thought, *at least once in a while when you really needed to get away. Lisa would love it, so would Mom and Dad. . . .*

It was strange how she wouldn't even think about him for days, then all of sudden, some little thing would remind her. And the hurt would start all over again. *Oh, Dad. I miss you so much. God, please let Gram help me find him. Please.*

"Jennie? Are you all right?"

"I'm fine." Jennie brushed the wetness from her cheeks with the back of her hand. "I was just thinking about Dad. He'd love it here."

"Yes, he would." Gram closed her computer and put it in the case. "We're almost there. We'll need to watch for a thirty-foot statue of a dolphin and her calf at the entrance."

"Gee, Gram, better keep a sharp eye out," she teased. "A statue that small will be hard to spot."

The Dolphin Research Center was almost the complete opposite of Dolphin Playland. There were no protesters and no elaborate gift shops, or lavish settings or auditoriums. It had a relaxed atmosphere with comfortable old buildings and open-air classrooms. A tour guide, who introduced himself as Mike, explained that they were a nonprofit organization. Mike walked them through the facility, explaining their various programs and introducing them to several dolphins. Like those Jennie had seen earlier, they performed elaborate dives and spirals and seemed to enjoy every minute of it.

When they were back in the car and on the road again, Jennie sipped on the cola she'd gotten at a market near the center and thought about the flyer Scott and Melissa had given her.

"You seem deep in thought," Gram said.

"This place is so different from Dolphin Playland. I mean, these people really care about the dolphins. Except for the ones that need medical care, the dolphins are here because they want to be. The other place . . . I don't know, it's so commercial."

"I sensed that too. I'm glad we were able to stop here." Gram took her computer out again. "It will be interesting to hear what Scott has to say."

Jennie glanced at Gram, then back at the road. "That's the second time you've mentioned him. How come you want to talk to Scott, anyway? He seems like an opinionated scuzzball."

"Scuzzball? You know, dear, in my day when a young lady resorted to name calling, it meant she had more than a passing interest. You know the old saying, 'Methinks thou dost protest too much.' Could it be that you're developing a crush on him?"

Jennie groaned. "No! He's definitely not my type. Anyway, what makes you so sure you'll be talking to him? He probably won't call you."

"Oh, he'll call. I think he likes you."

"Gram, be serious. I think you're getting me mixed up with Lisa. I'm Jennie, remember—the tall, skinny kid who spends most Saturday nights reading mysteries. My boyfriend, at least I thought he was my boyfriend, just turned down a date with me to go fishing."

"Jennie McGrady, is that any way to talk? You're a lovely girl. And as far as Ryan is concerned, going to Alaska was a hard decision for him. When he asked me about it I assured him you would understand. Was I wrong?"

Ryan lived on the coast in Bay Village and was Gram's next-door neighbor. He and Jennie had been friends a long time. In the last few weeks they'd grown closer. "No," she said reluctantly. "I even told him he should go. But it still hurts."

"Yes . . . yes, it does." Gram looked out the window, and Jennie had the feeling she was no longer talking about her or Ryan.

"Grandpa Ian left you like that too, didn't he, Gram?"

"What?" Gram looked surprised. "Now, how did you know I was thinking about him?"

Jennie shrugged her shoulders. "I just did."

"We'd only just fallen in love when he took a job with British Intelligence. World War II was in full swing and he came to me, wanting so much to go and so much to stay. I kissed him goodbye wondering if I'd ever see him again . . . there were so many casualties. Six months later he came back. We married, and well . . . you know the rest. It seemed like I was forever saying goodbye to that man."

"Gram, if Grandpa Ian had disappeared like Dad did, would you have gotten married to somebody else?"

"I don't know." Gram leaned over and patted Jennie's arm. "Now, don't be comparing me with your mother. We're as different as night and day."

"That's for sure." Mom was an accountant, Gram, a writer. Gram loved mystery, excitement, and adventure;

Mom loved security and a husband who came home every night.

"Being different doesn't make either of us wrong, Jennie. But enough of this maudlin conversation. This is a beautiful day, and we're heading for Key West."

Gram was right. Jennie once again took up her resolve to forget about all the conflicts going on in her life and concentrate on Florida and sunshine and having a great time.

Key West, Jennie discovered, was an island bulging with tourists. A friend of Gram's was visiting relatives in New York and had given them use of her home, a quaint Caribbean-style house that had been built in 1840 and recently restored. Since the house was only a few blocks from Old Town, they decided to walk to Mallory Square to have dinner and watch the sunset.

They were seated on the deck of what Jennie thought must be the world's classiest restaurant and had a spectacular view of the Gulf of Mexico. As they ate their meal of broiled swordfish, rice pilaf, and broccoli with hollandaise, bright orange and purple splashes of color covered the sky. Concerns about Ryan, Nick, her mom and Michael, and Dad had slipped into a fuzzy, remote corner of her mind. Several boats glided across the horizon, their dark sails silhouetted against the fiery sky.

"It's beautiful," Jennie whispered. "I wish I could stay here forever."

"Hmmm." Gram sipped her tea and smiled. "Moments like these are to be captured in the soul and relived in harder times."

They were just leaving the restaurant when a large dinner cruise ship approached the wharf area. "Let's watch," Jennie suggested. It had been a spectacular sunset, and the people aboard seemed flushed with excitement as they filed past Jennie and Gram. Jennie was about to dub the evening the most perfect one she'd ever had when a loud, raspy voice broke the quiet.

"If I ever catch you within a foot of my boats again I'll smack that big mouth of yours so hard you won't be able to eat for a month!" the voice boomed. "Now, get your gear and get out of here."

"But what about my pay? You owe me for four days . . ." That voice. Jennie had heard it before.

"You're lucky I don't sue you for thirty times that. Now, get out of here before I call the cops."

As soon as Jennie saw the shadowy figure emerge from the boat, she knew why the voice had sounded familiar. "Scott." She hadn't meant to say his name out loud and didn't realize she had until he spun around in her direction.

He stared at her for a moment and touched a hand to the cut above his eyebrow, then heaved a sigh and walked away. He was obviously embarrassed; Jennie knew the feeling well. "Wait," Jennie called. He didn't respond, so she ran after him. When she caught up with him about halfway down the block, Jennie wondered why she'd bothered.

"What do you want?" he snarled.

"I . . . I guess maybe I wanted to help. Though I'm not sure why. You are the rudest person I've ever met."

"Well, you're . . ." Scott's expression softened. "Look, I'm sorry. I guess I'm not in the greatest mood. I just got fired."

"I heard." Jennie tucked some hair that had escaped her braid behind her ear. "What happened?"

"I decked one of the passengers."

"You what? No wonder you got fired."

"The guy deserved it. He totally ignored the rules. Went diving and came up with a big chunk of live coral from the reef."

"How do you know it was live?"

"I saw him do it. When I tried to signal him not to, he just ignored me. We got into a big fight and I won."

"That's a matter of opinion," Jennie said as she pushed aside his hair to get a better look at the cut. He winced. "Your eye is swollen, and that cut looks like it needs stitches. What do you think, Gram?" When no one answered, Jennie felt her stomach knot in alarm. Jennie spun around. Gram wasn't there.

5

"You looking for the old lady who was with you at Dolphin Playland this afternoon?" Scott asked.

"She's not an old lady—she's my grandmother."

Scott shrugged. "Same difference."

"She was right behind me. At least I thought . . ."

"What are you getting so upset about? She looked like she could take care of herself."

"She can . . . but . . . oh, never mind. Just help me find her."

"Okay, let's go back to where you last saw her." Scott took hold of her shoulders. "And calm down. She's probably back on the wharf watching the sunset entertainment."

Jennie drew in a deep breath. "You're right. I'm calm. I know she was with me when we left the restaurant. We were watching the last of the sunset. Do you remember seeing her when you got off the boat?"

Scott shook his head. "No, I didn't notice. But that's a good place to start. C'mon." He took hold of her hand and pulled her forward. They wove their way through the crowd, and after what seemed an eternity, they reached the wharf where she'd last seen Gram.

"Where is she?" Panic streaked through her again.

Scott led her to a bench. "Let's just sit here and wait for her."

"Are you crazy? I can't do that. Someone may have kidnaped her . . ."

"What?" Scott shook his head. "I must be missing something here. Why in the world would anyone want to kidnap your grandmother?"

"Because she's a . . . *Nice going, McGrady. Why not announce it to the entire world while you're at it? Hey everyone . . . my grandmother is a secret agent. Works for the FBI in her spare time.*

"Let me guess," Scott leaned forward and placed an elbow on his knee. "She's filthy rich, and you're afraid someone has kidnaped her so they can collect a ransom."

"No." *Better make this good, McGrady.* "She's a writer. And she used to be a police officer."

"Oh, I get it." Scott slipped into a Sly Stallone accent—almost looked the part with his cut and bruised face. "She's made some enemies . . . she's testified against a mafia don, and now the mob's gonna fit her with a pair of cement boots."

"Close. Our flight out of Portland was canceled because of a bomb threat. Gram didn't think it had anything to do with her, but . . ."

Scott jumped to his feet. "Oh, man, I gotta get out of here."

Jennie glanced in the direction of the wharf. The man who'd fired Scott was stepping off his boat. "Scott, wait. He's not going to hurt you. Not with all these people around."

"Yeah, you're probably right. But that guy's a mean dude, and I'd just as soon not have my face messed up any more than it already is."

"Wow! Look." Jennie stared in disbelief as two uniformed policemen escorted the man into a nearby squad car. "You really don't have to worry about him. I wonder what happened."

Scott shrugged. "I don't know. Maybe you could ask your grandmother."

Helen McGrady emerged from the boat, talking animatedly to another officer. "I sure appreciate the call Mrs. McGrady. We've been trying to nail old Captain Nemo here for a long time. Only next time, how about giving us a call *first*?"

As they approached, Gram smiled. "Oh, Officer, here's the young man I was telling you about."

Scott stiffened. "What's this all about?"

"I was hoping you could tell me." The officer pulled a note pad from his back pocket.

"Hey, look, I didn't do anything." Scott lifted his hands and stepped back.

"Maybe I should explain." Gram adjusted her shoulder bag. "You see, Jennie and I overheard your boss threaten you, and then when you came off that boat looking as you did . . . well, I decided then and there to have a word with him. I thought perhaps I could persuade him to at least pay you your wages. While you and Jennie were talking, I went aboard. I was just about to go down the stairs into the cabin when I heard voices. It didn't take long to figure out what was going on. It seems your boss had a sideline."

"Right," the officer added. "Drug smuggling. Cocaine. A sweet setup. He takes tourists out for diving, dinner, and dancing, and when he arrives at the reef, sends a diver out to pick up the drop. We figure he either used someone posing as a tourist or his crew . . ."

Scott took a step back and collided with the bench. "I . . . I didn't know. Honest." He looked at Jennie then Gram. "I had nothing to do with it."

"Then you won't mind coming down to the station to answer a few questions."

When Jennie saw the look of fear in his eyes, she knew what he was thinking. *Don't run, Scott, please don't run.*

Gram must have sensed the same thing. "Why don't we all go together? I need to give my statement as well, and when we're finished there, we can have a doctor take a look at your eye."

An hour and a half later the police dropped Jennie, Gram, and Scott at the house. The three of them quickly piled into the car and headed for the hospital. Jennie stole glances at Scott through the rearview mirror. It made her nervous having him there, especially now that she knew he was a juvenile offender. He'd been arrested four times in the last year and a half. She felt certain Scott hadn't known about his boss's drug-smuggling operation, but it bothered her that Gram had been so trusting. She glanced back at him again. He met her gaze and gave her a sheepish grin before shifting his attention to Gram.

"Thanks again, Mrs. McGrady. If it hadn't been for you, I'd probably be in jail right now."

Gram turned sideways in her seat. "Yes, you would. I hope that in the future, when you're questioned by police, you'll refrain from calling them pigs and telling them where to go."

"Yeah, well, maybe they could quit harassing me. It seems like they're always trying to pin something on me. Even the dolphin killing. Just because I was working at Dolphin Playland when it happened . . ."

"You were working there?"

"For about two months last summer. They canned me after the dolphin died. They found out I was a volunteer with the DPA and accused me of killing their dolphin to make them look bad."

Jennie and Gram exchanged glances.

"Hey, I didn't do it."

"I'm sure you didn't," Gram offered. Jennie said nothing, concentrating instead on finding a parking place near the emergency-room entrance to the hospital.

It was midnight before they got home, and Jennie was not happy. Since Scott had been living on one of his boss's boats, he no longer had a place to stay. Gram, of course, had insisted he stay with them. Jennie filled the teakettle with water, slammed the kettle on the stove, and flipped on the burner. She could hear Gram and Scott talking in the living room where they were making up the sofa bed for him.

Ease up, McGrady, she told herself. *The guy's been through a lot. What did you want her to do, make him sleep on the street? Besides, you're the one who ran after him. Face it, McGrady. You're jealous because Gram is spending so much time helping him.*

"I am not jealous," she muttered, yanking open the cupboards above the stove. "Gram," she yelled. "Do you know where the tea is?"

"She's upstairs." Scott appeared behind her.

Jennie gasped and whirled around. "Good grief. You scared me half to death. How long have you been there?"

"Long enough." He leaned around her and lifted up a canister marked *TEA*. "You might look in here."

Jennie yanked the canister out of his hand, and in the process dumped the entire contents on the floor. "Now look what you made me do." Jennie dropped to the floor and started scooping the loose tea back into its container. She closed her eyes to hold back the threatening storm inside her.

Scott hunkered down beside her. "Do you want me to go?" When she didn't answer, he went on. "Hey, I can take a hint. I know you don't want me here. And if you really want me to leave, I will."

Jennie sat back on her heels and threw her long braid back over her shoulder. "Your eyes are the same color as my cousin Lisa's. 'Course she doesn't have a shiner."

"What kind of an answer is that?"

Jennie sighed. "I could never say no to her either."

Scott gave her a lopsided grin. "Does that mean what I think it does?"

"It means you can stay, but don't get any ideas." Jennie straightened and headed for the pantry to get a broom and dustpan.

When she emerged, Scott was standing by the door and she nearly ran into him. "What kind of ideas?" he asked, his voice low and husky. He reached behind her and flattened his palm on the doorjamb. Jennie met his gaze and forgot to breathe. Butterflies fluttered in her stomach. *He is going to kiss me.*

Not if she had anything to say about it. Jennie ducked under his arm and took a deep breath. "Those kind of ideas."

He shrugged his shoulders and smiled. "Just checking."

"Here . . ." She handed him the broom. "Why don't you finish cleaning this up while I find Gram?" At his questioning look she added, "Don't worry. I'm just going to ask her if we have any more tea."

After the others had gone to sleep, Jennie snuggled under her covers and, using the credit card Mom had given her, called home.

"Jennie, I'm so glad you called. I tried you several times tonight. I was getting worried."

"We were out for a while."

"Is everything all right? Your voice sounds odd."

Jennie thought about saying, *No, Mom, everything is not fine. We met this juvenile delinquent named Scott. He's got these incredible green eyes and brown curly hair and has been arrested four times. Gram busted up his boss's drug-smuggling scam, so you don't have to worry about that. But she invited Scott to stay with us, and he tried to kiss me.* Jennie smiled, imagining what her mother's reaction would have been if she'd actually said it. Mom would be on the next plane to Florida.

"Jennie," Mom asked again, "are you okay?"

"I'm fine, Mom. Just a little tired. Traveling with Gram is a little like being caught up in a windstorm."

"Well, you tell Gram to slow down and smell the roses. Oh, by the way, Ryan called."

Jennie popped up, suddenly alert. "He did? When? Why didn't he call here; did you give him the phone number? Did he leave a number where I could call him?"

Mom chuckled. "You don't like this guy or anything, do you?"

"Mom . . ."

"Okay, yes, he called—this afternoon. I gave him your number. He said he couldn't leave one because he was calling from a pay phone. He said he'd try to call you, but he only had a few minutes before the fishing boat left. He also said if he couldn't get you today, he'd try again in a few days."

42

"But we won't be here in a few days."

"Relax, honey, I gave him the number of the research center on Dolphin Island."

"Oh . . ." Jennie twisted the cord around her finger, trying to keep the disappointment she felt out of her voice. "Thanks, Mom. So . . . how's the kid? Did he get Coco?"

"No . . . but don't worry, I told him not to expect it until tomorrow. He's fine. Michael's been a lifesaver."

Jealousy nibbled at the edge of Jennie's thoughts, but she ignored it. "Have you heard from Lisa?"

"Oh, I'm glad you asked. She called today too. She asked me to have you call her the minute I heard from you."

"Did she say why?" Jennie glanced at the clock. With the three-hour time difference it would be about ten there. Lisa would still be up.

"No, only that it was important."

"Then, I guess I'd better hang up and call her. Give Nick a hug from me."

"I will. I love you."

"Love you too, Mom. Bye." Jennie waited for the dial tone and called Lisa. She answered on the first ring.

"Wow," Jennie said, "you must have been sitting on the phone."

"I was. Listen, you're not going to believe this."

"Let me guess. You and Brad are engaged."

"Get serious. No, listen. You know those people we overheard at the airport?"

"You mean Maggie and Tim?" Jennie leaned forward.

"Right. Well, I was looking for an article in the paper on the environment for Sociology, and there they were."

"Who?"

"Sarah and Maggie and that blond guy . . . the people we saw at the airport."

"You're kidding."

"Get this. Sarah's last name is Stanford. She's fourteen, and hasn't been able to talk since her dad died two years ago. Maggie, her mom, said she was taking her to Florida for a special kind of therapy where they use dolphins."

Excitement stirred in Jennie. "Did the paper say where they were going?"

Lisa giggled. "Just that the center is located near Fort Myers in a place called Dolphin Island."

6

"I can't believe it," Jennie squealed. "That's where we're going day after tomorrow." It looked as though she'd get to talk with Sarah and Maggie after all. "So tell me what else you found out. You said she hasn't talked for two years?"

"Right. Her father was John Stanford, a psychiatrist who was murdered a couple of years ago. Sarah was there when it happened."

"Wow. No wonder she looked scared." Jennie remembered the haunted look she'd seen in Sarah's eyes.

"Anyway, maybe Dr. Stanford was the guy Tim was talking about at the airport. Remember?"

"Yeah," Jennie tried to pull into focus the conversation she'd overheard. "Tim said something about Ramsey not killing John. Did the article say anything about that?"

"Just a minute . . . here's something. This is a quote from Dr. Layton. 'While the murder of my good friend and partner, Dr. John Stanford, has been resolved, his daughter's silence remains a mystery. It is our hope that Dr. Cole and her team of trained bottle-nose dolphins will be able to restore Sarah to the brilliant and vibrant child she once was.' "

"Does it say anything else about the murder?"

"No. It's mostly about Dr. Layton and using dolphins in therapy."

"He isn't Sarah's therapist, is he?" Jennie asked, remembering the way he'd kissed Maggie at the airport.

"He used to be until he and Maggie got married. Now he's her stepfather."

"Hmmm. If the murder was resolved, I wonder why Tim would think the bomb threat was meant for Sarah."

"I don't know, but I have the feeling you plan to find out."

Jennie thanked her cousin for the information, then after swearing her to secrecy, told her about Scott.

"Is he dangerous?" Lisa asked in a conspiratorial tone.

"I don't think so." Jennie flipped over on her stomach and shifted the phone to her other ear. "Gram said it was mostly a matter of his being in the wrong places at the wrong times. Unfortunately, his temper doesn't help."

"Well, be careful." Jennie heard Uncle Kevin's voice in the background yelling at Lisa to hang up. "Gotta go. Dad's having a cow."

Jennie turned out the light. Sleep eluded her as her mind kept dredging up pictures of Sarah. Those huge, dark, vacant eyes reminded Jennie of the starving children in Africa. She tried to imagine what it would have been like for Sarah to witness her father's murder. "Poor girl," Jennie murmured. "It must have been terrible for you."

Jennie's father hadn't been murdered, but she knew what it was like to lose a dad. Even though she'd never even met Sarah, Jennie felt connected with her. Despite the growing curiosity and excitement over seeing Sarah and Maggie again, jet lag and a full day's activity finally

46

pushed Jennie over the brink of wakefulness into a deep sleep.

The next morning Jennie joined Gram on the patio for breakfast. After pouring herself a glass of orange juice, Jennie told Gram about the article Lisa had found. "This is so weird," she said, scooping a piece of papaya out of its skin. "I mean . . . I don't even know Sarah and Maggie, but I can't stop thinking about them."

"And now it looks as though we'll be staying at the same place." Gram looked longingly at the plate of bacon and finally reached for a piece. "Perhaps you'll be able to help her in some tangible way after all, Jennie. We'll just have to wait and see what God brings about." Gram studied her bacon before finally taking a bite. "I really shouldn't be eating this. The doctor said I should be watching my cholesterol."

Jennie grinned. "You always say that and then you go right ahead and eat it."

"I do, don't I? It's my weakness."

Jennie helped herself to two pieces and handed the plate to Gram. "Want some more?"

"No, better save the rest for Scott. Which reminds me, have you seen him?"

Jennie frowned. "He's in the shower."

"Good," Gram said, "there's something I want to ask you about."

"You're wondering what we can do to get rid of him?" Jennie asked hopefully. As soon as the words left her mouth she wished she could have taken them back.

"Jennie, I'm disappointed in your attitude. I thought you wanted to help him."

"I'm sorry. I did want to help. I just . . ." Jennie glanced at her grandmother, then down at her half-eaten papaya. "I don't know. There's something about him that makes me uncomfortable. Anyway, what were you going to ask me?"

"I was going to ask what you thought of our inviting Scott to join us at Dolphin Island. I've already spoken to Kevin and Debbie Cole, the people who run the center, and they're willing to consider giving Scott a job."

"If you've already arranged it, why bother to ask my opinion?" Fighting back waves of anger, she pushed away from the table. "Maybe you ought to just send me home and finish your trip with Scott."

"I see." Gram calmly placed her napkin on the table.

Jennie swallowed hard. *Nice going, McGrady. Gram treats you like an adult and you act like a jealous three-year-old.* "I'm sorry," Jennie apologized again. "It's just that this was supposed to be *our* time—a chance for us to be together."

Gram surprised her by saying, "You're right. Here I invited you on this trip so we could spend some quality time together, and the first thing I do is to get involved in another cause. If you don't want him to come with us, that's fine." Gram paused and took a sip of tea. "Still, I'd like to help him . . ." She brightened. "We could give him money—enough to tide him over until he can get a job, or to buy a bus ticket home." She leaned toward Jennie. "What do you think?"

"Hey, guys . . . what's happening?" Scott approached the table, his hair still wet from his shower. He had on the same ragged cutoffs he'd worn during the protest the day before, only this morning he was wearing a T-shirt with a picture of a dolphin on the front and a caption that read *Born to Be Free*.

Scott sat down and helped himself to generous portions of scrambled eggs, bacon, and fresh fruit. "This looks great. My mom used to fix breakfast like this before . . ." Scott's eyes dimmed then brightened again, "Hey, you know, Mrs. McGrady, I was just thinking, since I don't have a job anymore, maybe I could show you and Jennie around today. I could take you out to the reef to go snorkeling . . . 'course you'd have to rent a boat . . ." He turned toward Jennie and shrugged. "Or, maybe you two would rather go alone."

Jennie expected Gram to jump in and tell Scott that they'd be delighted to have him show them around. When she didn't, Jennie realized Gram was waiting for her response. *Here's your chance, McGrady*, she told herself. *Tell him thanks, but no thanks*.

"That's really nice of you, Scott," she said. When she looked up and saw the lopsided grin on his face, the discomfort Jennie so often felt around him reappeared. *Face it, McGrady, the feelings you have for Scott have nothing to do with mistrust. You like the guy*. Jennie groaned. "I do not . . ." Then, realizing she'd said it out loud, added, ". . . think I can stand to go another minute without a shower."

Jennie pushed her chair away from the table. "While I'm getting ready, why don't you and Gram decide what we're going to do? Just be sure to leave some time free for hanging out at the beach."

All through the shower and during their sail out to the reef, Jennie thought about Scott. She had to admit that despite his faults, there was something appealing about him. He was definitely good-looking, and besides, who could resist those gorgeous green eyes? If Lisa were here she'd be standing next to him at the wheel, learning all about boats and diving. Lisa wouldn't think twice about flirting with him, even if she had another boyfriend. "Loosen up, Jennie," she'd say. "It's not like I'm going to marry him."

"You look deep in thought." Gram joined her at the railing and leaned against it.

"I am." Jennie turned around to face the wind and the water. "Have you ever liked two guys at the same time?"

Gram smiled. "You mean like Ryan and Scott?"

Jennie nodded. "It seems like I'm always getting on Lisa's case for being such a flirt. I really thought I loved Ryan, but we've only been apart for a couple of weeks, and I'm interested in Scott. It just doesn't seem right."

"Do you remember the little poems I used to share with you and Lisa when you two would disagree?"

Jennie nodded. "Lisa is like a butterfly. She flitters around from one place to another, and everywhere she goes people feel all the more blessed for her having been there."

"And do you remember yours?"

Jennie smiled. "An eagle, steady, strong, and to the point. She flies ever upward to touch the sky, blessing others with her strength."

"Lisa has her way of dealing with becoming a woman and being interested in the opposite sex. Now you'll need to find yours. In the meantime, why don't you try to relax and enjoy yourself? It's not every day we have an opportunity like this."

Jennie decided to take Gram's advice. She was an eagle, not a mole, and today seemed perfect for a new adventure. With Scott's help, Jennie and Gram learned the snorkeling basics. Scott carefully went over the rules and explained how fragile and vulnerable the coral reef ecosystem was.

"Most people don't realize it," Scott said, "but it can take years for some of these corals to grow one inch. Even touching the coral polyps can damage them."

After giving thorough instructions, Scott helped Jennie and Gram into their float coats and issued them masks and snorkels. Fully equipped, they descended the boat ladder and dropped into the water. At the reef they were greeted by some of the most colorful fish Jennie had ever seen. Their neon stripes flashed as they darted playfully in and out of the sea grass and coral. Scott pointed out a sea turtle and a queen conch, which he'd explained earlier was an endangered species. Jennie could understand why. Any shell collector would find it hard to pass up the beautiful seven-inch shell.

After what seemed like only a few minutes, Scott signaled them back to the boat. They'd been in the water for over an hour. During the sail back to Key West, they talked about the different species they'd seen, and identified them on a plastic chart Gram had purchased on the wharf.

As they approached the dock area, Jennie took Gram aside. "I've been thinking about your suggestion to ask Scott to come with us to Dolphin Island. We should ask him," Jennie said. "We must be good for him . . . at least you are. He's so different from when we first met him."

Gram nodded. "I could be wrong, but I think perhaps it's because we're offering him something he hasn't had in a long time."

Jennie frowned. "What?"

"Respect, friendship, a chance to prove himself. And maybe a feeling that someone cares about him. Last night when I asked him where he lived, he said his mom has a house in Orlando and his dad in Miami and that he lives somewhere in between."

51

"Oh, Gram. That is so sad."

"Yes. Yes, it is. What's worse is that he thinks neither of them wants him."

"So when are you going to ask him?"

"How about now?"

The surprise and excitement on Scott's face as Gram asked him about accompanying them up north and possibly working at the research center on Dolphin Island was all the thanks either of them needed to know they'd made the right decision.

When they got back to the house, Gram called the Coles to let them know Scott would be there. Scott called Melissa and told her he wouldn't be picketing Dolphin Playland for a while. During the rest of the afternoon and evening, Jennie sensed a change in Scott. After the phone call he seemed more subdued and maybe even a little nervous. Jennie began to wonder if he was having second thoughts.

After Gram had gone to bed, Jennie lingered in the living room, hoping he'd tell her what was bothering him. When he didn't, she asked. "You look upset about something. Have you changed your mind about coming? You don't have to, you know."

"You'd like that, wouldn't you?" he snapped. His bristling attitude reminded her of their first meeting.

"Hey, I don't care if you come or not. But if you do, at least try to act civilized. You've been sulking ever since that phone call you made to Melissa. Is she your girlfriend or something? Is she upset about you going?"

"No. She's real excited about my going up there. Thought it was a great opportunity."

Jennie leaned forward. "So what's the problem?"

Scott gave her a long, hard look. "You don't want to know." He stood and headed out the door. "Don't wait up."

7

Jennie felt a sudden sense of loss and guilt. Had she hurt his feelings by saying she didn't care whether or not he came? Or was it something else? Something to do with Melissa?

Jennie climbed the steps and paused at Gram's bedroom. Should she tell her Scott had gone? No. Scott hadn't taken his stuff, and that was a good sign. Maybe he just had to get away and think. There was no sense worrying her if that was the case.

But what if it isn't, McGrady? What if he doesn't come back? Jennie slipped under her covers and closed her eyes and did the only thing she could do. "God," she whispered, "keep Scott safe. And if you want him to come with us, then bring him back."

———

As it turned out, Jennie needn't have worried. Scott was up and packed at six A.M. Jennie flashed him a smile to let him know she was glad to see him. He greeted them both with a half-embarrassed, half-guilty grin and took their bags. They'd cleaned the house and set it in order the night before, and after Gram made a final check, they piled into the convertible and headed north. Gram took her turn at driving first and since she wanted to interview Scott, asked Jennie to sit in the back and take notes.

"Tell us how it all started, Scott," Gram said, after they'd settled in for the long drive. "What would cause a high-school boy to become such an avid environmentalist?"

"Actually, I've been interested in marine life for as long as I can remember. When I was about seven I saw this television special by Jacques Cousteau and decided then and there I was going to be a marine biologist when I grew up."

"You've been protesting since you were seven?" Jennie asked.

Scott shifted in his seat so he could talk to both Gram and Jennie. "No, I didn't get really involved until I decided to do a paper on dolphins. When I discovered how intelligent dolphins are and how well they relate to people, I decided I wanted to do something to help. I feel even stronger about it now that I've actually been in the water with them. There's something . . . it's hard to explain. It's like they know things."

"You mean like intuition?" Gram asked. "I've read some articles about how they've rescued people at sea."

"Yeah." Scott grew more animated as he talked. "But it's more than that. It's like they understand us. Anyway, you'll see what I mean when you get in the water with them."

"Scott," Gram said, "I can understand why you'd protest and lobby against senseless killing of the dolphins by fishermen, but why protest places like Dolphin Playland?"

"That place is the worst. Dolphins shouldn't be captured so they can entertain people at fancy resorts or per-